INDIANA JONES
AND THE
SPEAR OF DESTINY

PART ONE

SCRIPT & COLORS
Elaine Lee

PENCILS
Will Simpson

INKS
Dan Spiegle

LETTERS
Clem Robins

COVER ART
Hugh Fleming

DARK
HORSE
COMICS

Spotlight

VISIT US AT
www.abdopublishing.com

Reinforced library bound edition published in 2009 by Spotlight, a division of the ABDO Publishing Group, 8000 West 78th Street, Edina, Minnesota 55439. Spotlight produces high-quality reinforced library bound editions for schools and libraries. Published by agreement with Dark Horse Comics, Inc., and Lucasfilm Ltd.

Library of Congress Cataloging-in-Publication Data

Lee, Elaine.
  Indiana Jones and the Spear of Destiny / Elaine Lee, script, colors ; Will Simpson, pencils ; Dan Spiegle, inks ; Clem Robins, letters ; Hugh Fleming, cover art ; Teena Gores, publication design ; Bob Cooper & Dan Thorsland, edits. -- Reinforced library bound ed.
      p. cm. -- (Indiana Jones)
  "Dark Horse."
  ISBN 978-1-59961-577-6 (vol. 1)
  1. Graphic novels. [1. Graphic novels.] I. Simpson, Will, ill. II. Title.
  PZ7.7.L44In 2008
  [Fic]--dc22
                            2008009794

All Spotlight books have reinforced library bindings and are manufactured in the United States of America.